peg + cat

The Lemonade Problem

JENNIFER OXLEY
+ BILLY ARONSON

CANDLEWICK
ENTERTAINMENT

It was a hot day, but Peg and Cat were doing something very cool -- going into business!

They set up a lemonade stand
to sell ice-cold lemonade to thirsty people.

1 🥤 = 10 ⬡ ⦂⦂

5

2+1=3

The thirsty customers who bought their lemonade
would pay for it with marbles.

Peg couldn't wait to get more marbles
to put under her hat with her special marble.

Peg made a sign advertising
ONE cup of lemonade for TEN marbles.

3+1=4

"Very cool customers
headed this way!"
said Cat.

"It's the Teens,"
said Peg.
"And they're loaded
with marbles."

5+1=6

"Lemonade is so in
right now," said Tessa.

"But just **ONE** cup for **TEN** marbles?"
asked Mora.
"Sorry, Peg, but I can't spend
TEN marbles on **ONE** cup of lemonade.
I'm not made of marbles!"

The Teens skated away.

"Teens love to buy things, but they didn't buy our lemonade," said Peg.

"If they think **TEN** marbles is too much to pay for **ONE** cup of lemonade, let's sell **ONE** cup for **NINE** marbles. **NINE** is less than **TEN**."

Peg changed the sign.

But when the Teens returned, they left again without buying lemonade. The price was still too high.

6+1=7

"FIVE marbles is even less than NINE," said Peg, lowering the price again.

But the Teens still weren't buying. So Peg lowered the price one more time.

$1 \text{🥤} = 5$ •••••••

$1 \text{🥤} = 2$ ••

"Only TWO marbles for ONE cup of lemonade?" asked Mora.

"Sounds like something just went on sale!" said Tessa.

7+1=8

"I'm texting all my LLFs--

lemonade-loving friends!"

added Tessa.

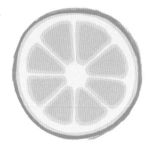

"Our business is on fire!"
said Peg.
"You can put ice in the cups, Cat,
and I'll pour the lemonade."

"Um, Peg?" asked Cat.
"Where are the cups?"

"The cups!" said Peg.
"I forgot the cups!"

"Hold on, Teens!"
shouted Peg.
They needed to find
some cups fast.

"Cat," said Peg,
"take these homemade
cookies that my mom made
over to Viv
and trade them
for **TWENTY** cups."

Cat took the cookies
and ran!

Viv was happy to trade cookies for cups--
but she only had TWO cups.

"TWO is almost TWENTY, right?" said Cat.

Viv drew a bar graph.
Cat could see that TWO was a lot less than TWENTY.

"I need someone with lots of cups!" said Cat.

"Mac at Mac's Flamenco Shack
has lots of cups," said Viv.

"But he doesn't care
for cookies.
So give the cookies
to me and I'll give you
these **TEN** red peppers.
Mac can really use peppers!"

Cat ran right over to Mac's.

13+1=14

"Welcome to Mac's Flamenco Shack,"
said Mac.

"Where the only thing better
than the food . . .

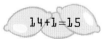

...is the dancing!"

Mac did a fast flamenco dance for Cat.

Cat cheered!

"The price for **ONE** dance
is **TEN** red peppers,"
said Mac.

Cat paid up.
Then he remembered that he
was supposed to use those peppers
to buy cups!

He stomped his foot
in frustration,
tripped,
knocked over a
bowl of fruit,
did a few backflips,
and landed.

Oomphf!

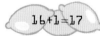
16+1=17

"What a great dance,"
said Mac.

"For doing it,
I'll pay you **TWO HUNDRED** cups!"

"Is **TWO HUNDRED** more than **TWENTY?**"
asked Cat.

"Way more," said Mac.
He showed **TWO HUNDRED** cups
and **TWENTY** cups on a chart
so that Cat could compare.

17+1=18

Meanwhile, Peg was doing
a song and dance about lemonade
to keep the Teens from leaving.

Suddenly Cat came back . . .

with LOTS of cups!

"Cat, you business genius!" said Peg.
"The lemonade is ready to flow!"

"Sweet!" said Jesse.

CRACKLE!

BOOM!

Gray storm clouds gathered overhead.
Thunder rumbled.

"Let's go before it rains on our marbles,"
said Mora, and the Teens left.

Nobody was thirsty for lemonade anymore.

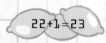

22+1=23

"What just happened?" said Cat.

"They wanted our lemonade," said Peg.
"Then the weather changed,
and now they don't want it."

Peg and Cat were frustrated.

And disappointed.

And TOTALLY FREAKING OUT!

23+1=24

Ramone arrived with
a flamenco flourish.

"Olé!"

He was on his way
to Mac's Flamenco Shack
to perform.

"Want some lemonade?"
asked Peg.

"How much is it?"
asked Ramone.

25+1=26

"I love lemonade!
Thanks, Peg!" said Ramone.

"By the way, I have something for you," said Ramone.
"This marble I found.
I thought you'd like it."

Peg loved the marble.
"It's smooth. And cool. And shiny!" she said.
"A perfect match for my special marble."

The clouds parted and the sun came back out.

The Teens came back out, too.

"Now I'm, like, sooo thirsty,"
said Mora.

"How many marbles for a cup of lemonade?"
asked Tessa.

Since the Teens were really thirsty, Peg was about to
ask for **TEN** marbles, or even more, for **ONE** cup of lemonade.
Then she had a better idea.

$$1 \, \boxed{} = 2 \, \bullet\bullet$$

"I don't need any more marbles," she said. "So . . .
free lemonade for everyone!"

30+1=31

This book is based on the TV series *Peg + Cat*.
Peg + Cat is produced by The Fred Rogers Company.
Created by Jennifer Oxley and Billy Aronson.
The Lemonade Problem is based on a television script co-written with David Peth
and background art by Amy De Lay, Erica Kepler, and Michael Zodorozny.
The PBS KIDS logo is a registered mark of the Public Broadcasting Service
and is used with permission.

pbskids.org/peg

First paperback edition 2018

Library of Congress Catalog Card Number 2017931935
ISBN 978-0-7636-9436-4 (hardcover)
ISBN 978-1-5362-0061-4 (paperback)

18 19 20 21 22 23 APS 10 9 8 7 6 5 4 3 2 1

Printed in Humen, Dongguan, China

This book was typeset in OPTITypewriter.
The illustrations were created digitally.

Candlewick Entertainment
an imprint of Candlewick Press
99 Dover Street
Somerville, Massachusetts 02144

visit us at www.candlewick.com